ALFRED BULLTOP STORMALONG

RETOLD BY EMILY DOLBEAR ⚓ ILLUSTRATED BY KATHLEEN PETELINSEK

The Child's World®
childsworld.com

Published by The Child's World®
1980 Lookout Drive • Mankato, MN 56003-1705
800-599-READ • www.childsworld.com

ISBN 9781503850064 (Reinforced Library Binding)
ISBN 9781503851023 (Portable Document Format)
ISBN 9781503851788 (Online Multi-user eBook)
LCCN: 2021930082

Printed in the United States of America

ALFRED BULLTOP STORMALONG

Long ago in this young country, Alfred Bulltop Stormalong started life in New England near the sea. It was most surely on the hooked sandy peninsula of Massachusetts people call Cape Cod. But there's a slight chance it was Maine, up north a bit. The one thing every living soul knows, without a doubt, is this celebrated adventurer came from there or somewhere else.

Thing is, Alfred Bulltop Stormalong was born as big as his name was long. No jokin', he measured two fathoms from tip to baby toe. That's twelve feet to landlubbers like you and me. And that was before he got to growin'. Everyone called him Stormy, though he was good natured and calm as could be.

Now Stormy loved every nook, cranny, and krill of the salty sea he lived so near. He swam its frigid water. He ate its scallops and bluefish. And he sailed like silk over its choppy whitecaps. You see, Stormy didn't always fit in on land. On account of his height, that gray ocean was the only place he felt peaceful.

Soon Stormy had grown to more than six fathoms. Or perhaps it could possibly have been twelve. Whatever the number, it added up to mighty tall.

"Stormy, you tower so," his mother said one day as she tucked him into bed. "We need to poke another hole in the roof."

And on it went. He swapped in a broom for his toothbrush and a rake for his comb. His chowder spoon could dig up the front garden. Once, after a whopping sneeze, his pop, a cheerful seafarer, offered his son a mainsail to wipe his nose.

When he turned eighteen, Stormy decided to ship out as a cabin boy. He signed on with a schooner headed for China. His family waved him off. He waved back, standing neither starboard nor port side so as not to tip anything over.

Stormy fit right in with the ragtag crew. He fixed the mast rigging without even shinnying. He looked ahead for dangerous weather by just standing up. But one sunny morning, the ship came to a sudden halt in the middle of the ocean.

"Hey, ho! A sea creature has taken hold of our keel!" shouted the captain.

In a flash, Stormy leapt overboard. Two seconds later, he popped up and jumped back on deck. The boat bolted forward again in the water.

"It was just an octopus," Stormy explained. "We wrestled, and I tied its limbs into a few bowlines. What's for lunch?"

A few years on and Stormy began to tire of the seafaring life. He still felt like a giant of sorts. So he returned to shore and headed west. Over his shoulder, he swung an old wooden oar. I'm going to walk, he thought to himself, until no one knows what's on my shoulder. Then, I'll know I'm free of the sea.

So walk Stormy did, miles and miles, until he reached the Great Plains of Kansas. And if it wasn't Kansas, it was most likely Utah. Wherever it may have been, no farmer there had any idea why he carried that long stick on his shoulder. Right at that spot, Stormy planted his first crop.

You may know where this tale is headin'. Sure enough, after a couple harvests, Alfred Bulltop Stormalong heard a faint calling from the ocean. Memories of the vast sea, his kind family, and plentiful fish chowder brought him to tears. People say when his tears fell, they created the Great Salt Lake. If Utah was where he was.

When he returned back East at last, Stormy removed his trusty oar from his shoulder. Then he jumped in the ocean, makin' a wave that rippled all the way to Portugal and back. He drank in the salty sea as if it were the freshest water he'd ever tasted.

After suppin' with his family, Stormy left to travel the world on a clipper ship. He sailed all seven seas, a few bays, and a fjord or two. They say he captained a ship 'round the Cape Horn in South America, pushing the icebergs aside with his foot.

All the while, Stormy stood tall and proud in his very own ship. That's right, a ship built just for him. The masts reached so high, they almost knocked the Big Dipper out of the sky. But it was fast as a horse, so he dubbed it the *Courser*.

On one of Stormy's last voyages, the *Courser* got stuck like a cork in a bottle. It was in the English Channel, the watery path between France and Dover, England. They could go neither forward nor back. Only way out, as Stormy saw it, was to soap up the sides and drive the ship through.

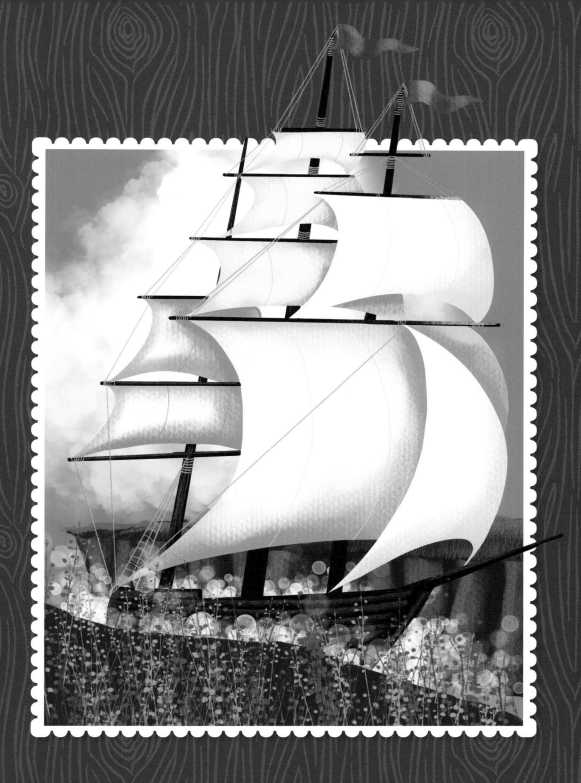

"More suds!" Captain Stormalong ordered his crew from the poop deck.

Those able-bodied sailors furiously lathered the hull until the ship could pass. My sakes, if those black cliffs of Dover didn't turn white that day and for all time.

Today, sailors, able bodied, put the letters *A.B.* after their names, some say to remember Alfred Bulltop. They also honor him with a shanty, which they sing as they work. "Old Stormy's dead and gone to rest," it goes. "Of all the sailors, he was the best."

A.B.

BEYOND THE STORY

Have you ever heard of a real infant twelve feet long at birth? Of course not. This is a tall tale, or a greatly exaggerated story. And the story of the outsize Alfred Bulltop Stormalong is certainly a *tall* tale.

Tall tales mix some facts about history with imaginative storytelling. They usually include a larger-than-life character like Alfred Bulltop Stormalong. This particular American folk tale doesn't seem to be based on an actual person. But in the first half of the nineteenth century, many real adventurers sailed on wooden trading ships from New England to China, just as Stormy did.

There are different versions of this tall tale. Some say Stormy was born after a single hurricane wave crashed ashore, leaving behind an enormous infant sitting in a pile of seaweed. Other versions focus on Stormy's healthy appetite. His breakfast consisted of six sharks or a dozen ostrich eggs, or both. He drank fish soup out of a boat and cider from a fire hose.

This tall tale may have originated in the 1830s or 1840s as a sea shanty called "Old Stormalong." Sea shanties are traditional folk songs. Sailors sang them together for fun or to help synchronize their work rigging sails or scrubbing the decks.

The rhythm of a sea shanty can be catchy, even to today's listeners. At the end of 2020, a young Scotsman posted a short video of himself singing one. It got millions of views around the world.

ABOUT THE AUTHOR

Emily Dolbear lives with her family in the great state of Massachusetts, though she's put down roots in a few other places. She eats fish chowder by the bucketful, she startles almost never by bulls charging, not once has she grown taller than her father, and she follows her own nose.

ABOUT THE ILLUSTRATOR

Kathleen Petelinsek has loved to read and draw since she was a child. She lives near a small town in southern Minnesota with her husband, two dogs, one kitty, and three chickens.